WITCH FROM HELL'S KITCHEN

BY

ROBERT E. HOWARD

British Library Cataloguing-in-Publication Data
A catalogue record for this book is available from the
British Library

Robert E. Howard

Robert Ervin Howard was born in Peaster, Texas in 1906. During his youth, his family moved between a variety of Texan boomtowns, and Howard – a bookish and somewhat introverted child – was steeped in the violent myths and legends of the Old South. Although he loved reading and learning, Howard developed a distinctly Texan, hardboiled outlook on the world. He became a passionate fan of boxing, taking it up at an amateur level, and from the age of nine began to write adventure tales of semi-historical bloodshed. In 1919, when Howard was thirteen, his family moved to the Central Texas hamlet of Cross Plains, where he would stay for the rest of his life.

At fifteen Howard began to read the pulp magazines of the day, and to write more seriously. The December 1922 issue of his high school newspaper featured two of his stories, 'Golden Hope Christmas' and 'West is West'. In 1924 he sold his first piece – a short caveman tale titled 'Spear and Fang' – for $16 to the not-yet-famous *Weird Tales* magazine. He published with the magazine regularly over the next few years. 1929 was a breakout year for Howard, in that the 23-year-old writer began to sell to other magazines, such as *Ghost Stories* and *Argosy*, both of whom had previously sent him hundreds of rejection slips. In 1930, he began a correspondence with weird fiction master H. P. Lovecraft which ran up to his death six years later, and is regarded as one of the great correspondence cycles in all of fantasy literature.

It was partly due to Lovecraft's encouragement that Howard created his most famous character, Conan the Cimmerian. Conan – a barbarian-turned-King during the Hyborian Age, a mythical period of some 12,000 years ago – featured in seventeen *Weird Tales* stories between 1933 and 1936, and is now regarded as having spawned the 'sword and sorcery' genre, making Howard's influence on fantasy literature comparable to that of J. R. R. Tolkien's. The Conan stories have since been adapted many times, most famously in the series of films starring Arnold Schwarzenegger.

Howard was enjoying an all-time high in sales by the beginning of 1936, but he was also deeply upset by the ill health of his mother, who had fallen into a coma. On the morning of June 11, 1936, he asked an attending nurse whether she would ever recover, and the nurse replied negatively. Howard walked to his car, parked outside the family home in Cross Plains, and shot himself. He died eight hours later, aged just thirty.

To the house whence no one issues,
To the road from whence there is no return,
To the house whose inhabitants are deprived of light,
The place where dust is their nourishment, their food
clay,
They have no light, dwelling in dense darkness,
And they are clothed, like birds, in a garment of feathers,
Where, over gate and bolt, dust is scattered.
-Babylonian legend of Ishtar

"HAS HE seen a night-spirit, is he listening to the whispers of them who dwell in darkness?"

Strange words to be murmured in the feast-hall of Naram-ninub, amid the strain of lutes, the patter of fountains, and the tinkle of women's laughter. The great hall attested the wealth of its owner, not only by its vast dimensions, but by the richness of its adornment. The glazed surface of the walls offered a bewildering variegation of colors-blue, red, and orange enamels set off by squares of hammered gold. The air was heavy with incense, mingled with the fragrance of exotic blossoms from the gardens without. The feasters, silk-robed nobles of Nippur, lounged on satin cushions, drinking wine poured from alabaster vessels, and caressing the painted and bejeweled playthings which Naramninub's wealth had brought from all parts of the East.

There were scores of these; their white limbs twinkled as they danced, or shone like ivory among the cushions where they sprawled. A jeweled tiara caught in a burnished mass of night-black hair, a gem-crusted armlet of massive gold, earrings of carven jade-these were their only garments. Their fragrance was dizzying. Shameless in their dancing, feasting and lovemaking, their light laughter filled the hall in waves of silvery sound.

On a broad cushion-piled dais reclined the giver of the feast, sensuously stroking the glossy locks of a lithe Arabian who had stretched herself on her supple belly beside him. His appearance of sybaritic languor was belied by the vital sparkling of his dark eves as he surveyed his guests. He was thick-bodied, with a short blue-black beard: a Semite one of the many drifting yearly into Shumir.

With one exception his guests were Shumirians, shaven of chin and head. Their bodies were padded with rich living, their features smooth and placid. The exception among them stood out in startling contrast. Taller than they, he had none of their soft sleekness. He was made with the economy of relentless Nature. His physique was of the primitive, not of the civilized athlete. He was an incarnation of Power, raw, hard, wolfish-in the sinewy limbs, the corded neck, the great arch of the breast, the broad hard shoulders. Beneath his tousled golden mane his eyes were like blue ice. His strongly chiseled features reflected the wildness his frame suggested. There was about him nothing of the measured leisure of the other guests, but a ruthless directness in his every action. Whereas they sipped, he drank in great gulps. They nibbled at tid-bits, but he seized whole joints in his fingers and tore at the meat with his teeth. Yet his brow was shadowed, his expression moody. His magnetic eyes were introspective. Wherefore Prince Ibi-Engur lisped again in Naram-ninub's ear: "Has the lord, Pyrrhas, heard the whispering of night-things?"

Naram-ninub eyed his friend in some worriment. "Come, my lord," said he, "you are strangely distraught. Has any here done aught to offend you?"

Pyrrhas roused himself as from some gloomy meditation and shook his head. "Not so, friend; if I seem distracted it is because of a shadow that lies over my own mind." His accent was barbarous, but the timbre of his voice was strong and vibrant.

The others glanced at him in interest. He was Eannatum's general of mercenaries, an Argive whose saga was epic.

"Is it a woman, lord Pyrrhas?" asked Prince Enakalli with a laugh. Pyrrhas fixed him with his gloomy stare and the prince felt a cold wind blowing on his spine.

"Aye, a woman," muttered the Argive. "One who haunts my dreams and floats like a shadow between me and the moon. In my dreams I feel her teeth in my neck, and I wake to hear the flutter of wings and the cry of an owl."

A silence fell over the group on the dais. Only in the great hall below rose the babble of mirth and conversation and the tinkling of lutes, and a girl laughed loudly, with a curious note in her laughter.

"A curse is upon him," whispered the Arabian girl. Naram-ninub silenced her with a gesture, and was about to speak, when Ibi-Engur lisped: "My lord Pyrrhas, this has an uncanny touch, like the vengeance of a god. Have you done aught to offend a deity?"

Naram-ninub bit his lip in annoyance. It was well known that in his recent campaign against Erech, the Argive had cut down a priest of Anu in his shrine. Pyrrhas' maned head jerked up and he glared at Ibi-Engur as if undecided whether to attribute the remark to malice or lack of tact. The prince began to pale, but the slim Arabian rose to her knees and caught at Naramninub's arm.

"Look at Belibna!" She pointed at the girl who had laughed so wildly an instant before.

Her companions were drawing away from this girl apprehensively. She did not speak to them, or seem to see them. She tossed her jeweled head and her shrill laughter rang through the feast-hall. Her slim body swayed back and forth, her bracelets clanged and jangled together as she tossed up her white arms. Her dark eves gleamed with a wild light, her red lips curled with her unnatural mirth.

"The hand of Arabu is on her," whispered the Arabian uneasily.

"Belibna?" Naram-ninub called sharplv. His only answer was another burst of wild laughter, and the girl cried stridently: "To the home of darkness, the dwelling of Irhalla; to the road whence there is no return; oh, Apsu, bitter is thy wine!" Her voice snapped in a terrible scream, and bounding from among her cushions, she leaped up on the dais, a dagger in her hand. Courtesans and guests shrieked and scrambled madly out of her way. But it was at Pyrrhas the girl rushed, her beautiful face a mask of fury. The Argive caught her wrist, and the abnormal strength of madness was futile against the barbarian's iron thews. He tossed her from him, and down the cushion-strewn steps, where she lay in a crumpled heap, her own dagger driven into her heart as she fell.

The hum of conversation which had ceased suddenly, rose again as the guards dragged away the body, and the painted dancers came back to their cushions. But Pyrrhas turned and taking his wide crimson cloak from a slave, threw it about his shoulders.

"Stay, my friend," urged Naram-ninub. "Let us not allow this small matter to interfere with our revels. Madness is common enough."

Pyrrhas shook his head irritably. "Nay, I'm weary of swilling and gorging. I'll go to my own house."

"Then the feasting is at an end," declared the Semite, rising and clapping his hands. "My own litter shall bear you to the house the lung has given you-nay, I forgot you scorn the ride on other men's backs. Then I shall myself escort you home. My lords, will you--accompany us?"

"Walk, like common men?" stuttered Prince Ur-ilishu. "By Enlil, I will come. It will be a rare novelty. But I must have a slave to bear the train of my robe, lest it trail in the dust of the street. Come, friends, let us see the lord Pyrrhas home, by Ishtar!"

"A strange man," Ibi-Engur lisped to Libit-ishbi, as the party emerged from the spacious palace, and descended the broad tiled stair, guarded by bronze lions. "He walks the streets, unattended, like a very tradesman."

"Be careful," murmured the other. "He is quick to anger, and he stands high in the favor of Eannatum."

"Yet even the favored of the king had best beware of offending the god Ann," replied Ibi-Engur in an equally guarded voice.

The party were proceeding leisurely down the broad white street, gaped at by the common folk who bobbed their shaven heads as they passed. The sun was not long up, but the people of Nippur were well astir. There was much coming and going between the booths where the merchants spread their wares: a shifting panorama, woven of craftsmen, tradesmen, slaves, harlots, and soldiers in copper helmets. There went a merchant from his warehouse, a staid figure in sober woolen robe and white mantle; there hurried a slave in a linen tunic; there minced a painted hoyden whose short slit skirt displayed her sleek flank at every step. Above them the blue of the sky whitened with the heat of the mounting sun. The glazed surfaces of the buildings shimmered. They were flatroofed, some of them three or four stories high. Nippur was a city of sun-dried brick, but its facings of enamel made it a riot of bright color.

Somewhere a priest was chanting: "Oh, Babbat, righteousness lifteth up to thee its head-"

Pyrrhas swore under his breath. They were passing the great temple of Enlil, towering up three hundred feet in the changeless blue sky.

"The towers stand against the sky like part of it," he swore, raking back a damp lock from his forehead. "The sky is enameled, and this is a world made by man."

"Nay, friend," demurred Naram-ninub. "Ea built the world from the body of Tiamat."

"I say men built Shumir!" exclaimed Pyrrhas, the wine he had drunk shadowing his eves. "A flat land--a very banquetboard of a land--with rivers and cities painted upon it, and a sky of blue enamel over it. By Ymir, I was born in a land the gods built! There are great blue mountains, with valleys lying like long shadows between, and snow peaks glittering in the sun. Rivers rush foaming down the cliffs in everlasting tumult, and the broad leaves of the trees shake in the strong winds."

"I, too, was born in a broad land, Pyrrhas," answered the Semite. "By night the desert lies white and awful beneath the moon, and by day it stretches in brown infinity beneath the sun. But it is in the swarming cities of men, these hives of bronze and gold and enamel and humanity, that wealth and glory lie."

Pyrrhas was about to speak, when a loud wailing attracted his attention. Down the street came a procession, bearing a carven and painted litter on which lay a figure hidden by flowers. Behind came a train of young women, their scanty garments rent, their black hair flowing wildly. They beat their naked bosoms and cried: "Ailanu! Thammuz is dead!" The throngs in the street took up the shout. The litter passed, swaying on the shoulders of the bearers; among the high-piled flowers shone the painted eyes of a carven image. The cry of the worshipers echoed down the street, dwindling in the distance.

Pyrrhas shrugged his mighty shoulders. "Soon they will be leaping and dancing and shouting, 'Adonis is living!', and the wenches who howl so bitterly now will give themselves to men in the streets for exultation. How many gods are there, in the devil's name?"

Naram-ninub pointed to the great zikkurat of Enlil, brooding over all like the brutish dream of a mad god.

"See ye the seven tiers: the lower black, the next of red enamel, the third blue, the fourth orange, the fifth yellow, while the sixth is faced with silver, and the seventh with pure gold which flames in the sunlight? Each stage in the temple symbolizes a deity: the sun, the moon, and the five planets Enlil and his tribe have set in the skies for their emblems. But Enlil is greater than all, and Nippur is his favored city."

"Greater than Anu?" muttered Pyrrhas, remembering a flaming shrine and a dying priest that gasped an awful threat.

"Which is the greatest leg of a tripod?" parried Naramninub.

Pyrrhas opened his mouth to reply, then recoiled with a curse, his sword flashing out. Under his very feet a serpent reared up, its forked tongue flickering like a jet of red lightning.

"What is it, friend?" Naram-ninub and the princes stared at him in surprise.

"What is it?" He swore. "Don't you see that snake under your very feet? Stand aside--and give me a clean scaring at it."

His voice broke off and his eyes clouded with doubt.

"It's gone," he muttered.

"I saw nothing," said Naram-ninub, and the others shook their heads, exchanging wondering glances.

The Argive passed his hand across his eyes, shaking his head.

"Perhaps it's the wine," he muttered. "Yet there was an adder, I swear by the heart of Ymir. I am accursed."

The others drew away from him, glancing at him strangely.

Them had always been a restlessness in the soul of Pyrrhas the Argive, to haunt his dreams and drive him out on his long wanderings. It had brought him from the blue mountains of his race, southward into the fertile valleys and seafringing plains where rose the huts of the Mycenaeans; thence into the isle of Crete, where, in a rude town of rough stone and wood, a swart fishing people bartered with the ships of Egypt; by those ships he had gone into Egypt, where men toiled beneath the lash to rear the first pyramids, and where, in the ranks of the white-skinned mercenaries, the Shardana, he learned the arts of war. But his wanderlust drove him again across the sea, to a mudwalled trading village on the coast of Asia, called Troy, whence he drifted southward into the pillage and carnage of Palestine where the original dwell--in the land were trampled under by the barbaric Canaanites out of the East. So by devious ways he came at last to the plains of Shumir, where city fought city, and the priests of a myriad rival gods intrigued and plotted, as they had done since the dawn of Time, and as they did for centuries after, until the rise of an obscure frontier town called Babylon exalted its city-god Merodach above all others as Bel-Marduk, the conqueror of Tiamat.

The bare outline of the saga of Pyrrhas the Argive is weak and paltry; it can not catch the echoes of the thundering pageantry that rioted through that saga: the feasts, revels, wars, the crash and splintering of ships and the onset of chariots. Let it suffice to say that the honor of kings was given to the Argive, and that in all Mesopotamia here was no man so feared as this golden-haired barbarian whose war-skill and fury broke the hosts of Erech on the field, and the yoke of Erech from the neck of Nippur.

From a mountain but to a palace of jade and ivory Pyrrhas' saga had led him. Yet the dim half-animal dreams that had filled his slumber when he lay as a youth on a heap of wolfskins in his shaggy-headed father's but were nothing so strange and monstrous as the dreams that haunted him on the silken couch in the palace of turquoise-towered Nippur.

It was from these dreams that Pyrrhas woke suddenly. No lamp burned in his chamber and the moon was not yet up, but the starlight filtered dimly through the casement. And in this radiance something moved and took form. There was the vague outline of a lithe form, the gleam of an eye. Suddenly the night beat down oppressively hot and still. Pyrrhas heard the pound of his own blood through his veins.

Why fear a woman lurking in his chamber? But no woman's form was ever so pantherishly supple; no woman's eyes ever burned so in the darkness. With a gasping snarl he leaped from his couch and his sword hissed as it cut the air-but only the air. Something like a mocking laugh reached his ears, but the ure was gone.

A girl entered hastily with a lamp.

"Amytis! I saw her! It was no dream, this time! She laughed at me from the window!"

Amytis trembled as she set the lamp on an ebony table. She was a sleek sensuous creature, with long-lashed, heavy-lidded eyes, passionate lips, and a wealth of lustrous black curly locks. As she stood there naked the voluptuousness of her figure would have stirred the most jaded debauchee. A gift from Eannatum, she hated Pyrrhas, and he knew it, but found an angry gratification in possessing her. But now, her hatred was drowned in her terror.

"It was Lilitu!" she stammered. "She has marked you for her own! She is the night-spirit, the mate of Ardat Lili. They dwell in the House of Arabu. You are accursed!"

His hands were bathed with sweat; molten ice seemed to be flowing sluggishly through his veins instead of blood.

"Where shall I turn? The priests hate and fear me since I burned Anu's temple."

"There is a man who is not bound by the priest-craft, and could aid you." She blurted out.

"Then tell me!" He was galvanized, trembling with eager impatience. "His name, girl! His name!"

But at this sign of weakness, her malice returned; she had blurted out what was in her mind, in her fear of the supernatural. Now all the vindictiveness in her was awake again.

"I have forgotten," she answered insolently, her eyes glowing with spite.

"Slut!" Gasping with the violence of his rage, he dragged her across a couch by her thick locks. Seizing his swordbelt he wielded it with savage force, holding down the writhing naked body with his free hand. Each stroke was like the impact of a drover's whip. So mazed with fury was he, and she so incoherent with pain, that he did not at first realize that she was shrieking a name at the top of her voice. Recognizing this at last, he cast her from him, to fall in a whimpering heap on the mat-covered floor. Trembling and panting from the excess of his passion, he threw aside the belt and glared down at her.

"Gimil-ishbi, eh?"

"Yes!" she sobbed, groveling on the floor in her excruciating anguish. "He was a priest of Enlil, until he turned diabolist and was banished. Ahhh, I faint! I swoon! Mercy! Mercy!"

"And where shall I find him?" he demanded.

"In the mound of Enzu, to the west of the city. Oh, Enlil, I am flayed alive! I perish!"

Turning from her, Pyrrhas hastily donned his garments and armor, without calling for a slave to aid him. He went forth, passed among his sleeping servitors without waking them, and secured the best of his horses. There were perhaps a score in all in Nippur, the property of the king and his wealthier nobles; they had been bought from the wild tribes far to the north, beyond the Caspian, whom in a later age men called Scythians. Each steed represented an actual fortune. Pyrrhas bridled the great beast and strapped on the saddle--merely a cloth pad, ornamented and richly worked.

The soldiers at the gate gaped at him as he drew rein and ordered them to open the great bronze portals, but they bowed and obeyed without question. His crimson cloak flowed behind him as he galloped through the gate.

"Enlil!" swore a soldier. "The Argive has drunk overmuch of Naram-ninub's Egyptian wine."

"Nay," responded another; "did you see his face that it was pale, and his hand that it shook on the rein? The gods have touched him, and perchance he rides to the House of Arabu."

Shaking their helmeted heads dubiously, they listened to the hoof-beats dwindling away in the west.

North, south and east from Nippur, farm-hues, villages and palm groves clustered the plain, threaded by the net-

16

works of canals that connected the rivers. But westward the land lay bare and silent to the Euphrates, only charred expanses telling of former villages. A few moons ago raiders had swept out of the desert in a wave that engulfed the vineyards and huts and burst against the staggering walls of Nippur. Pyrrhas remembered the fighting along the walls, and the fighting on the plain, when his sally at the head of his phalanxes had broken the besiegers and driven them in headlong flight back across the Great River. Then the plain had been red with blood and black with smoke. Now it was already veiled in green again as the grain put forth its shoots, uncared for by man. But the toilers who had planted that grain had gone into the land of dusk and darkness.

Already the overflow from more populous districts was seeping; back into the man-made waste. A few months, a year at most, and the land would again present the typical aspect of the Mesopotamian plain, swarming with villages, checked with tiny fields that were more like gardens than farms. Man would cover the scars man had made, and there would be forgetfulness, till the raiders swept again out of the desert. But now the plain lay bare and silent, the canals choked, broken and empty.

Here and there rose the remnants of palm groves, the crumbling ruins of villas and country palaces. Further out, barely visible under the stars, rose the mysterious hillock known as the mound of Enzu--the moon. It was not a natural hill, but whose hands had reared it and for what reason none knew. Before Nippur was built it had risen above the plain, and the nameless fingers that shaped it had vanished in the dust of time. To it Pyrrhas turned his horse's head.

And in the city he had left, Amytis furtively left his palace and took a devious course to a certain secret destination. She walked rather stiffly, limped, and frequently paused to tenderly caress her person and lament over her injuries. But limping, cursing, and weeping, she eventually reached her destination, and stood before a man whose wealth and power was great in Nippur. His glance was an interrogation.

"He has gone to the Mound of the Moon, to speak with Gimil-ishbi," she said.

"Lilitu came to him again tonight," she shuddered, momentarily forgetting her pain and anger. "Truly he is accursed."

"By the priests of Anu?" His eyes narrowed to slits.

"So he suspects."

"And you?"

"What of me? I neither know nor care."

"Have you ever wondered why I pay you to spy upon him?" he demanded.

She shrugged her shoulders. "You pay me well; that is enough for me."

"Why does he go to Gimil-ishbi?"

"I told him the renegade might aid him against Lilitu."

Sudden anger made the man's face-.darkly sinister.

"I thought you hated him."

She shrank from the menace in the voice. "I spoke of the diabolist before I thought, and then he forced me to speak his name curse him, I will not sit with ease for weeks!" Her resentment rendered her momentarily speechless.

The man ignored her, intent on his own somber meditations. At last he rose with sudden determination.

"I have waited too long," he muttered, like one speaking his thoughts aloud. "The fiends play with him while I bite my nails, and those who conspire with me grow restless and suspicious. Enlil alone knows what counsel Gimil-ishbi will give. When the moon rises I will ride forth and seek the Argive on the plain. A stab unaware--he will not suspect until my sword is through him. A bronze blade is surer than the powers of Darkness. I was a fool to trust even a devil."

Amytis gasped with horror and caught at the velvet hangings for support.

"You? You?" Her lips framed a question too terrible to voice.

"Aye!" He accorded her a glance of grim amusement. With a gasp of terror she darted through the curtained door, her smarts forgotten in her fright.

19

Whether the cavern was hollowed by man or by Nature, none ever knew. At least its walls, floor and ceiling were symmetrical and composed of blocks of greenish stone, found nowhere else in that level land. Whatever its cause and origin, man occupied it now. A lamp hung from the rock roof, casting a weird light over the chamber and the bald pate of the man who sat crouching over a parchment scroll on a stone table before him. He looked up as a quick sure footfall sounded on the stone steps that led down into his abode. The next instant a tall figure stood framed in the doorway.

The man at the stone table scanned this figure with avid interest. Pyrrhas wore a hauberk of black leather and copper scales; his brazen greaves glinted in the lamplight. The wide crimson cloak, flung loosely about him, did not enmesh the long hilt that jutted from its folds. Shadowed by his horned bronze helmet, the Argive's eyes gleamed icily. So the warrior faced the sage.

Gimil-ishbi was very old. There was no leaven of Semitic blood in his withered veins. His bald head was round as a vulture's skull, and from it his great nose jutted like the beak of a vulture. His eyes were oblique, a rarity even in a pure-blooded Shumirian, and they were bright and black as beads. Whereas Pyrrhas' eyes were all depth, blue deeps and changing clouds and shadows, Gimilishbi's eyes were opaque

20

as jet, and they never changed. His mouth was a gash whose smile was more terrible than its snarl.

He was clad in a simple black tunic, and his feet, in their cloth sandals, seemed strangely deformed. Pyrrhas felt a curious twitching between his shoulder-blades as he glanced at those feet, and he drew his eyes away, and back to the sinister face.

"Deign to enter my humble abode, warrior," the voice was soft and silky, sounding strange from those harsh thin lips. "I would I could offer you food and drink, but I fear the food I eat and the wine I drink would find little favor in your sight." He laughed softly as at an obscure jest.

"I come not to eat or to drink," answered Pyrrhas abruptly, striding up to the table. "I come to buy a charm against devils."

"To buy?"

The Argive emptied a pouch of gold coins on the stone surface; they glistened dully in the lamplight. Gimil-ishbi's laugh was like the rustle of a serpent through dead grass.

"What is this yellow dirt to me? You speak of devils, and you bring me dust the wind blows away."

"Dust?" Pyrrhas scowled. Gimil-ishbi laid his hand on the shining heap and laughed; somewhere in the night an owl moaned. The priest lifted his hand. Beneath it lay a pile of yellow dust that gleamed dully in the lamplight. A sudden wind rushed down the steps, making the lamp flicker, whirling up the golden heap; for an instant the air was dazzled and spangled with the shining particles. Pyrrhas swore; his armor was sprinkled with yellow, dust; it sparkled among the scales of his hauberk.

"Dust that the wind blows away," mumbled the priest. "Sit down, Pyrrhas of Nippur, and let us converse with each other."

Pyrrhas glanced about the narrow chamber; at the even stacks of clay tablets along the walls, and the rolls of papyrus above them. Then he seated himself on the stone bench opposite the priest, hitching his sword-belt so that his hilt was well to the front.

"You are far from the cradle of your race," said Gimil-ishbi. "You are the first golden-haired rover to tread the plains of Shumir."

"I have wandered in many lands," muttered the Argive, "but may the vultures pluck my bones if I ever saw a race so devil-ridden as this, or a land ruled and harried by so many gods and demons."

His gaze was fixed in fascination on Gimil-ishbi's hands; they were long, narrow, white and strong, the hands of youth. Their contrast to the priest's appearance of great age otherwise, was vaguely disquieting.

"To each city its gods and their priests," answered Gimil-ishbi; "and all fools. Of what account are gods whom the fortunes of men lift or lower? Behind all gods of men, behind the primal trinity of Ea, Ann and Enlil, lurk the elder gods, unchanged by the wars or ambitions of men. Men deny what they do not see. The priests of Eridu, which is sacred to Ea and light, are no blinder than them of Nippur, which is consecrated to Enlil, whom they deem the lord of Darkness. But he is only the god of the darkness of which men dream, not the real Darkness that lurks behind all dreams, and veils the real and awful deities. I glimpsed this truth when I was a priest of Enlil, wherefore they cast me forth. Ha! They would stare if they knew how many of their worshipers creep forth to me by night, as you have crept."

"I creep to no man!" the Argive bristled instantly. "I came to buy a charm. Name your price, and be damned to you."

"Be not wroth," smiled the priest. "Tell me why you have come."

"If you are so cursed wise you should know already," growled the Argive, unmollified. Then his gaze clouded as he cast back over his tangled trail. "Some magician has cursed me." he muttered. "As I rode back from my triumph over Erech, my scar-horse screamed and shied at Something none saw but he. Then my dreams grew strange and monstrous. In the darkness of my chamber, wings rustled and feet padded stealthily. Yesterday a woman at a feast went mad and tried to knife me. Later an adder sprang out of empty air and struck at me. Then, this night, she men call Lilitu came to my chamber and mocked me with awful laughter-"

"Lilitu?" the priest's eyes lit with a brooding fire; his skull-face worked in a ghastly smile. "Verily, warrior, they plot thy ruin in the House of Arabu. Your sword can not prevail against her, or against her mate Ardat Lili. In the gloom of midnight her teeth will find your throat. Her laugh will blast your ears, and her burning kisses will wither you like a dead leaf blowing in the hot winds of the desert. Madness and dissolution will be your lot, and you will descend to the House of Arabu whence none returns."

Pyrrhas moved restlessly, cursing incoherently beneath his breath.

"What can I offer you besides gold?" he growled.

"Much!" the black eyes shone; the mouth-gash twisted in inexplicable glee. "But I must name my own price, after I have given you aid."

Pyrrhas acquiesced with an impatient gesture.

"Who are the wisest men in the world?" asked the sage abruptly.

"The priests of Egypt, who scrawled on yonder parchments," answered the Argive.

Gimil-ishbi shook his head; his shadow fell on the wall like that of a great vulture, crouching over a dying victim.

"None so wise as the priests of Tiamat, who fools believe died long ago under the sword of Ea. Tiamat is deathless; she reigns in the shadows; she spreads her dark wings over her worshipers."

"I know them not," muttered Pyrrhas uneasily.

"The cities of men know them not; but the waste-places know them, the reedy marshes, the stony deserts, the hills, and the caverns. To them steal the winged ones from the House of Arabu."

"I thought none came from that House," said the Argive.

"No human returns thence. But the servants of Tiamat come and go at their pleasure."

Pyrrhas was silent, reflecting on the place of the dead, as believed in by the Shumirians; a vast cavern, dusty, dark and silent, through which wandered the souls of the dead forever, shorn of all human attributes, cheerless and loveless, remembering their former lives only to hate all living men, their deeds and dreams.

"I will aid you," murmured the priest. Pyrrhas lifted his helmeted head and stared at him. Gimil-ishbi's eyes were no more human than the reflection of firelight on subterranean pools of inky blackness. His lips sucked in as if he gloated over all woes and miseries of mankind: Pyrrhas hated him as a man hates the unseen serpent in the darkness.

"Aid me and name your price," said the Argive.

Gimil-ishbi closed his hands and opened them, and in the palms lay a gold cask, the lid of which fastened with a jeweled catch. He sprung the lid, and Pyrrhas saw the cask was filled with grey dust. He shuddered without knowing why.

"This ground dust was once the skull of the first king of Ur," said Gimil-ishbi. "When he died, as even a necromancer must, he concealed his body with all his art!! But I found his crumbling bones, and in the darkness above them, I fought with his soul as a man fights with a python in the night. My spoil was his skull, that held darker secrets than those that lie in the pits of Egypt."

"With this dead dust shall you trap Lilitu. Go quickly to an enclosed place-a cavern or a chamber-nay, that ruined villa which lies between this spot and the city will serve. Strew the dust in thin lines across threshold and window; leave not a spot as large as a man's hand unguarded. Then lie down as if in slumber. When Lilitu enters, as she will, speak the words I shall teach you. Then you are her master, until you free her again by repeating the conjure backwards. You can not slay her, but you can make her swear to leave you in peace. Make her swear by the dugs of Tiamat. Now lean close and I will whisper the words of the spell."

Somewhere in the night a nameless bird cried out harshly; the sound was more human than the whispering of the priest, which was no louder than the gliding of an adder through slimy ooze. He drew back, his gash-mouth twisted in a grisly smile. The Argive sat for an instant like a statue of bronze. Their shadows fell together on the wall with the appearance of a crouching vulture facing a strange horned monster.

Pyrrhas took the cask and rose, wrapping his crimson cloak about his somber figure, his horned helmet lending an illusion of abnormal height.

"And the price?"

Gimil-ishbi's hands became claws, quivering with lust.

"Blood! A life!"

"Whose life?"

"Any life! So blood flows, and there is fear and agony, a spirit ruptured from its quivering flesh! I have one price for all-a human life! Death is my rapture; I would glut my soul on death! Man, maid, or infant. You have sworn. Make good your oath! A life! A human life!"

"Aye, a life!" Pyrrhas' sword cut the air in a flaming arc and Gimil-ishbi's vulture head fell on the stone table. The body reared upright, spouting black blood, then slumped across the stone. The head rolled across the surface and thudded dully on the floor. The features stared up, frozen in a mask of awful surprise.

Outside there sounded a frightful scream as Pyrrhas' stallion broke its halter and raced madly away across the plain.

From the dim chamber with its tablets of cryptic cuneiforms and papyri of dark hieroglyphics, and from the remnants of the mysterious priest, Pyrrhas fled. As he climbed the carven stair and emerged into the starlight he doubted his own reason.

Far across the level plain the moon was rising, dull red; darkly lurid. Tense heat and silence held the land. Pyrrhas felt cold sweat thickly beading his flesh; his blood was a sluggish current of ice in his veins; his tongue clove to his palate. His armor weighted him and his cloak was like a clinging snare. Cursing incoherently he tore it from him; sweating and shaking he ripped off his armor, piece by piece, and cast it away. In the grip of his abysmal fears he had reverted to the primitive. The veneer of civilization vanished. Naked but for loin-cloth and girded sword he strode across the plain, carrying the golden cask under his arm.

No sound disturbed the waiting silence as he came to the ruined villa whose walls reared drunkenly among heaps of rubble. One chamber stood above the general ruin, left practically untouched by some whim of chance. Only the door had been wrenched from its bronze hinges. Pyrrhas entered. Moonlight followed him in and made a dim radiance inside the portal. There were three windows, gold-barred. Sparingly he crossed the threshold with a thin grey line. Each casement he served in like manner. Then tossing aside the empty cask, he stretched himself on a bare dais that stood in deep shadow. His unreasoning horror was under control. He who had been the hunted was now the hunter.

The trap was set, and he waited for his prey with the patience of the primitive.

He had not long to wait. Something threshed the air outside and the shadow of great wings crossed the moon lit portal. There was an instant of tense silence in which Pyrrhas heard the thunderous impact of his own heart against his ribs. Then a shadowy form framed itself in the open door. A fleeting instant it was visible, then it vanished from view. The thing had entered; the night-fiend was in the chamber.

Pyrrhas' hand clenched on his sword as he heaved up suddenly from the dais. His voice crashed in the stillness as he thundered the dark enigmatic conjurement whispered to him by the dead priest. He was answered by a frightful scream; there was a quick stamp of bare feet, then a heavy fail, and something was threshing and writing in the shadows on the floor. As Pyrrhas cursed the masking darkness, the moon thrust a crimson rim above a casement, like a goblin peering into a window, and a molten flood of light crossed the floor. In the pale glow the Argive saw his victim.

But it was no were-woman that writhed there. It was a thing like a man, lithe, naked, dusky-skinned. It differed not in the attributes of humanity except for the disquieting suppleness of its limbs, the changeless glitter of its eyes. It grovelled as in mortal agony, foaming at the mouth and contorting its body into impossible positions.

With a blood-mad yell Pyrrhas ran at the figure and plunged his sword through the squirming body. The point rang on the tiled floor beneath it, and an awful howl burst from the frothing lips, but that was the only apparent effect of the thrust. The Argive wrenched forth his sword and glared astoundedly to see no stain on the steel, no wound on the dusky body. He wheeled as the cry of the captive was re-echoed from without.

Just outside the enchanted threshold stood a woman, naked, supple, dusky, with wide eyes blazing in a soulless face. The being on the floor ceased to writhe, and Pyrrhas' blood turned to ice.

"Lilitu!"

She quivered at the threshold, as if held by an invisible boundary. Her eyes were eloquent with hate; they yearned awfully for his blood and his life. She spoke, and the effect of a human voice issuing from that beautiful unhuman mouth was more terrifying than if a wild beast had spoken in human tongue.

"You have trapped my mate! You dare to torture Ardat Lili, before whom the gods tremble! Oh, you shall howl for this! You shall be torn bone from bone, and muscle from muscle, and vein from vein! Loose, him! Speak the words and set him free, lest even this doom be denied you!"

"Words!" he answered with bitter savagery. "You have hunted me like a hound. Now you can not cross that line without falling into my hands as your mate has fallen. Come into the chamber, bitch of darkness, and let me caress you as I caress your lover-thus! and thus! and thus!"

Ardat Lili foamed and howled at the bite of the keen steel, and Lilitu screamed madly in protest, beating with her hands as at an invisible barrier.

"Cease! Cease! Oh, could I but come at you! How I would leave you a blind, mangled cripple! Have done! Ask what you will, and I will perform it!"

"That is well," grunted the Argive grimly. "I can not take this creature's life, but it seems I can hurt him, and unless you give me satisfaction, I will give him more pain than ever he guesses exists in the world."

"Ask! Ask!" urged the were-woman, twisting with impatience.

"Why have you haunted me? What have I done to earn your hate?"

"Hate?" she tossed her head. "What are the sons of men that we of Shuala should hate or love? When the doom is loosed, it strikes blindly."

"Then who, or what, loosed the doom of Lilitu upon me?"

"One who dwells in the House of Arabu."

"Why, in Ymir's name?" swore Pyrrhas. "Why should the dead hate me?" He halted, remembering a priest who died gurgling curses.

31

"The dead strike at the bidding of the living. Someone who moves in the sunlight spoke in the night to one who dwells in Shuala."

"Who?"

"I do not know."

"You lie, you slut! It is the priests of Anu, and you would shield them. For that lie your lover shall howl to the kiss of the steel--"

"Butcher!" shrieked Lilitu. "Hold your hand! I swear by the dugs of Tiamat my mistress, I do not know what you ask. What are the priests of Anu that I should shield them? I would rip up all their bellies-as I would yours, could I come at you! Free my mate, and I will lead you to the House of Darkness itself, and you may wrest the truth from the awful mouth of the dweller himself, if you dare!"

"I will go," said Pyrrhas, "but I leave Ardat Lili here as hostage. If you deal falsely with me, he will writhe on this enchanted floor throughout all eternity."

Lilitu wept with fury, crying: "No devil in Shuala is crueller than you. Haste, in the name of Apsu!"

Sheathing his sword, Pyrrhas stepped across the threshold. She caught his wrist with fingers like velvet-padded steel, crying something in a strange inhuman tongue. Instantly the moon-lit sky and plain were blotted out in a rush of icy blackness. There was a sensation of hurtling through a void of intolerable coldness, a roaring in the Argive's ears as of titan winds. Then his feet struck solid ground; stability followed that chaotic instant, that had been like the instant of dissolution that joins or separates two states of being, alike in stability, but in kind more alien than day and night. Pyrrhas knew that in that instant he had crossed an unimaginable gulf, and that he stood on shores never before touched by living human feet.

Lilitu's fingers grasped his wrist, but he could not see her. He stood in darkness of a quality which he had never encountered. It was almost tangibly soft, all-pervading and all-engulfing. Standing amidst it, it was not easy even to imagine sunlight and bright rivers and grass singing in the wind. They belonged to that other world - a world lost and forgotten in the dust of a million centuries. The world of life and light was a whim of chance-a bright spark glowing momentarily in a universe of dust and shadows. Darkness and silence were the natural state of the cosmos, not light and the noises of Life. No wonder the dead hated the living, who disturbed the grey stillness of Infinity with their tinkling laughter.

Lilitu's fingers drew him through abysmal blackness. He had a vague sensation as of being in a titanic cavern, too huge for conception. He sensed walls and roof, though he did not see them and never reached them; they seemed to recede as he advanced, yet there was always the sensation of their presence. Sometimes his feet stirred what he hoped was only dust. There was a dusty scent throughout the darkness; he smelled the odors of decay and mould.

He saw lights moving like glow-worms through the dark. Yet they were not lights, as he knew radiance. They were most like spots of lesser gloom, that seemed to glow only by contrast with the engulfing blackness which they emphasized without illuminating. Slowly, laboriously they crawled through the eternal night. One approached the companions closely and Pyrrhas' hair stood up and he grasped his sword. But Lilitu took no heed as she hurried him on. The dim spot glowed close to him for an instant; it vaguely illumined a shadowy countenance, faintly human, yet strangely birdlike.

Existence became a dim and tangled thing to Pyrrhas, wherein he seemed to journey for a thousand years through the blackness of dust and decay, drawn and guided by the hand of the were-woman. Then he heard her breath hiss through her teeth, and she came to a halt.

Before them shimmered another of those strange globes of light. Pyrrhas could not tell whether it illumined a man or a bird. The creature stood upright like a man, but it was clad in grey feathers-at least they were more like feathers than anything else. The features were no more human than they were birdlike.

"This is the dweller in Shuala which put upon you the curse of the dead," whispered Lilitu. "Ask him the name of him who hates you on earth."

"Tell me the name of mine enemy!" demanded Pyrrhas, shuddering at the sound of his own voice, which whispered drearily and uncannily through the unechoing darkness.

The eyes of the dead burned redly and it came at him with a rustle of pinions, a long gleam of light springing into its lifted hand. Pyrrhas recoiled, clutching at his word, but Lilitu hissed: "Nay, use this!" and he felt a hilt thrust into his fingers. He was grasping a scimitar with a blade curved in the shape of the crescent moon, that shone like an arc of white fire.

He parried the bird-thing's stroke, and sparks showered in the gloom, burning him like bits of flame. The darkness clung to him like a black cloak; the glow of the feathered monster bewildered and baffled him. It was like fighting a shadow in the maze of a nightmare. Only by the fiery gleam of his enemy's blade did he keep the touch of it. Thrice it sang death in his ears as he deflected it by the merest fraction, then his own crescent-edge cut the darkness and grated on the other's shoulder-joint. With a strident screech the thing dropped its weapon and slumped down, a milky liquid spurting from the gaping wound. Pyrrhas lifted his scimitar again, when the creature gasped in a voice that was no more human than the grating of wind-blown boughs against one another: "Naram-ninub, the great-grandson of my greatgrandson! By black arts he spoke and commanded me across the gulfs!"

"Naram-ninub!" Pyrrhas stood frozen in amazement; the scimitar was torn from his hand. Again Lilitu's fingers locked on his wrist. Again the dark was drowned in deep blackness and howling winds blowing between the spheres.

He staggered in the moonlight without the ruined villa, reeling with the dizziness of his transmutation. Beside him Lilitu's teeth shone between her curling red lips. Catching the thick locks clustered on her neck, he shook her savagely, as he would have shaken a mortal woman.

"Harlot of Hell! What madness has your sorcery instilled in my brain?"

"No madness!" she laughed, striking his hand-aside. "You have journeyed to the House of Arabu, and you have returned. You have spoken with and overcome with the sword of Apsu, the shade of a man dead for long centuries."

"Then it was no dream of madness! But Naram-ninub--" he halted in confused thought. "Why, of all the men of Nippur, he has been my staunchest friend!"

"Friend?" she mocked. "What is friendship but a pleasant pretense to while away an idle hour?"

"But why. in Ymir's name?"

"What are the petty intrigues of men to me?" she exclaimed angrily. "Yet now I remember that men from

36

Erech, wrapped in cloaks steal by night to Naramninub's palace."

"Ymir!" like a sudden blaze of light Pyrrhas saw reason in merciless clarity. "He would sell Nippur to Erech, and first he must put me out of the way, because the hosts of Nippur cannot stand before me! Oh, dog, let my knife find your heart!"

"Keep faith with me!" Lilitu's importunities drowned his fury. "I have kept faith with you. I have led you where never living man has trod, and brought you forth unharmed. I have betrayed the dwellers in darkness and done that for which Tiamat will bind me naked on a white-hot grid for seven times seven days. Speak the words and free Ardat Lili!"

Still engrossed in Naram-ninub's treachery, Pyrrhas spoke the incantation. With a loud sigh of relief, the were-man rose from the tiled floor and came into the moonlight. The Argive stood with his hand on his sword and his head bent, lost in moody thought. Lilitu's eyes flashed a quick meaning to her mate. Lithely they began to steal toward the abstracted man. Some primitive instinct brought his head up with a jerk. They were closing in on him, their eyes burning in the moonlight, their fingers reaching for him. Instantly he realized his mistake; he had forgotten to make them swear truce with him; no oath bound them from his flesh.

With feline screeches they struck in, but quicker yet he bounded aside and raced toward the distant city. Too hotly eager for his blood to resort to sorcery, they gave chase. Fear winged his feet, but close behind him he heard the swift patter of their feet, their eager panting. A sudden drum of hoofs sounded in front of him, and bursting through a tattered grove of skeleton palms, he almost caromed against a rider, who rode like the wind, a long silvery glitter in his hand. With a startled oath the horseman wrenched his steed back on its haunches. Pyrrhas saw looming over him a powerful body in scale mail, a pair of blazing eyes that glared at him from under a domed helmet, a short black beard.

"You dog!" he yelled furiously. "Damn you, have you come to complete with your sword what your black magic began?"

The steed reared wildly as he leaped at its head and caught its bridle. Cursing madly and fighting for balance, Naram-ninub slashed at his attacker's head, but Pyrrhas parried the stroke and thrust upward murderously. The sword-point glanced from the corselet and plowed along the Semite's jaw-bone. Naram-ninub screamed and fell from the plunging steed, spouting blood. His leg-bone snapped as he pitched heavily to earth, and his cry was echoed by a gloating howl from the shadowed grove.

Without dragging the rearing horse to earth, Pyrrhas sprang to its back and wrenched it about. Naram-ninub was groaning and writhing on the ground, and as Pyrrhas looked, two shadows darted from the darkened grove and fastened themselves on his prostrate form. A terrible scream burst from his lips, echoed by more awful laugher. Blood on the night air; on it the night-things would feed, wild as mad dogs, making no difference between men.

The Argive wheeled away, toward the city, then hesitated, shaken by a fierce revulsion. The level land lay quiescent beneath the moon, and the brutish pyramid of Enlil stood up in in the stars. Behind him lay his enemy, glutting the fangs of the horrors he himself had called up from the Pits. The road was open to Nippur, for his return.

His return?-to a devil-ridden people crawling beneath the heels of priest and king; to a city rotten with intrigue and obscene mysteries; to an alien race that mistrusted him, and a mistress that hated him.

Wheeling his horse again, he rode westward toward the open lands, flinging his arms wide in a gesture of renunciation and the exultation of freedom. The weariness of life dropped from him like a cloak. His mane floated in the wind, arid over the plains of Shumir shouted a sound they had never heard before-the gusty, elemental, reasonless laughter of a free barbarian.

THE END

www.ingramcontent.com/pod-product-compliance
Lightning Source LLC
Chambersburg PA
CBHW030241180626
46810CB00008B/3239